THE Boy
from
méxico

An Immigration Story
of Bravery and Determination

Written & Illustrated by
Edward A. Dennis

The art for this book was created using Corel® Painter®.

Author & Illustrator: Edward Dennis
Layout designer: Lilia Garvin

Published by DragonFruit, an imprint of Mango Publishing, a division of Mango Publishing Group, Inc.

For permission requests, please contact the publisher at:

Mango Publishing Group
2850 Douglas Road, 4th Floor
Coral Gables, FL
33134 USA
info@mango.bz

For special orders, quantity sales, course adoptions and corporate sales, please email the publisher at sales@mango.bz. For trade and wholesale sales, please contact Ingram Publisher Services at customer.service@ingramcontent.com or +1.800.509.4887.

The Boy from Mexico: An Immigration Story of Bravery and Determination

Library of Congress Cataloging-in-Publication number: 2022942639
ISBN: (p) 978-1-64250-983-0 (e) 978-1-64250-984-7
BISAC: JUV030100, JUVENILE FICTION / People & Places / Mexico

Corel®
Painter®

This book is dedicated to all the people who come to the United States in hopes of providing a better future for themselves and their families.

We live on a beautiful planet with countless magnificent places.

But...not ALL places
in el mundo are equal!

Many people feel they need to leave their homes...

just so their families can have a chance to be happy.

One of those people
was a boy named Luz.

He dreamed of making a better
life for himself and his familia.

While most fourteen-year-olds were playing with their friends,

Luz was plotting a path to the United States.

TIJUANA

SONORAN

DESERT CHIHUAHUAN

DESERT

SIERRA
MADRE MOUNTAINS

Michoacan

OCEANO PACIFICO

Someone who made the journey
once before gave him a map.

MEXICO

It looked impossible but...

Luz could not stay in his pueblo.

If he did, he'd never find out if the stories he heard about America were true.

They told him that in the United States,

anyone could become

anything!

At dinner, Luz decided to tell his familia of his decision to leave.

The family disagreed with his choice at first. His padre tried unsuccessfully to make the journey years ago.

But they knew Luz was **destined** for **something more.**

Saying adiós to his little hermano Pedro was not easy...

¡Buenos días!

Departing from the barrio, Luz took one last look.

He wondered when he'd
see his gente again.

Leaving his pueblo, he walked down a path he had walked before with his amigos.

He nervously looked back at everything he knew and realized...

no amigos this time,
and no family.

He was
all alone.

the trip had seemed
like an **adventure**
at first...

But he soon
realized how

BIG

the world was.

Luz's Casa

aro

But then, a few
days after the
boy left home,
he ran out of food.

Good thing his padre Ácatl
had taught him how to survive off
the land of Mexico.

Yum, nopal!

Luz's favorite meal.

On his tenth day, a massive storm came down the montañas verdes.

It seemed as if the storm was trying to force him to **go back**.

the water rushed by him like a raging river!

He was cold
and wet,
but Luz

Kept going.

He encountered animals and plants he had never seen before.

To help with his loneliness,
he would name all the creatures!

Coati

tapir

Acorn Weevil

Every night on his journey...

Luz would dream of los **Estados Unidos.**

He wondered
what it was really like.
Would they accept
and understand him?
It made him **nervous.**

On the twenty-first day of his journey, his feet were covered in painful red blisters and hurt so much he could hardly walk.

He wondered if he had made a mistake! He missed his familia **so much!**

Just then a couple pulled up in a truck.

they offered Luz a ride to the
next town on his map!

This was the farthest Luz had ever been from everything he knew.

He was scared but determined.

His fear turned to shock
as the familiar green land
became brown desert.

The nice couple gave Luz money for food and a bus ride to the last city on his map.

He was happy he would have time
to rest his feet the next day.

He celebrated his fifteenth birthday on the bus to Tijuana.

He was happy he didn't have to walk, but he missed the birthday fiestas his familia would throw.

they were full of comida deliciosa

and música!

Luz was now on the
last part of his journey.

He was in an environment
he had never been to before.

He was so close, but he did not expect

many things the desert had to offer.

The HEAT!

Luz had to run tree to tree to avoid the sun.

the pain brought out
every emotion Luz had
from the journey.

Getting across the border was just as difficult and frightening as getting to it!

Luz knew how **fortunate** he was to make it this far.

He wasn't going to waste this chance he was given.

Walking by the beach he realized the stories he heard in his pueblo were **true.**

Want to learn more about Luz and Mexican culture?
Check out the next few pages!

Facts about Mexico

Mexico is home to many different kinds of people. Many are descendants of indigenous peoples. These include the Olmecs, Toltecs, Totonacs, Zapotecs, Mixtecs, Mayans, and Aztecs. Many Mexicans are mixed with European people who colonized the area. There are also close to 3 million Afro-Mexicans in Mexico as well.

Mexican food is also varied. For many years, the people of Mexico have made food from maíz. The land of Mexico itself is diverse too, from northern deserts to ancient pyramids of Yucatán, Teotihuacán, and El Tajín. The land continues all the way past the rain forests to the beautiful beaches that tourists visit each year. Mexicans speak many indigenous languages in addition to Spanish. Lastly, Mexico is known for its vibrant art and música.

Glossary

Abuelita: grandmother

Ácatl: Mayan for reed

Adiós: goodbye

Amigos: friends

Barrio: neighborhood

Buenos días: good morning

Casa: house

Comida deliciosa: delicious food

El mundo: world

Familia: family

Fiestas: parties

Gente: people

Hermano: brother

Los Estados Unidos: The United States

Luz: light

Madre: mother

Maíz: corn

Montañas verdes: green mountains

Música: music

Océano Pacífico: Pacific Ocean

Nopal: cactus

Padre: father

Pedro: Peter

Pueblo: town

Tortuga: turtle

Y: and

Immigration facts

36 percent of unaccompanied immigrant children have at least one parent in the United States.

The United States was built by immigrants, starting with the first Europeans who moved onto Native American lands in the 1500s.

In the 1900s, the largest groups of immigrants came from Spanish-speaking countries in Latin America, especially Mexico.

When people immigrate, they leave behind their friends, families, and sometimes their culture. They also have to sell what they have that is too big to bring.

Immigration is the process of moving to a new country, with plans to live there permanently.

Questions for reflection

Why do some people like Luz choose to immigrate to other countries?

How do you think Luz's culture could help enrich the lives of non-Mexican people?

Have you ever seen anything in your everyday life that represented Mexican culture?

What are some ways we could make Luz feel comfortable in his new country if we met him?

Where are some other places people emigrate from other than Mexico?

Acknowledgements

This book would not be possible without those who inspired or helped, including my late mother who always made sure her son had what he needed to make his art and stories. She would read to me every night as a child and empowered me to believe that one day I could do whatever I wanted. My uncle Andy, who put the spirit of dreaming big in me at an early age and bought me my first art table and pencil set. My Abuelita Virgina and Abuelo George, for telling me I was an artist when I was only drawing stick figures. My father, who taught me perseverance, discipline, and that failure is how we grow. My third-grade teacher, for hanging up my artwork in the class. My high school art teacher, for always giving me honest feedback on my artwork. To my ancestors, who came before me from Mexico and didn't have the opportunities I have—I hope I'm making you proud.

About Luz

Luz Andres was born and raised just outside the city of Patzcuaro, Mexico. When Luz isn't working with his padre he likes to play soccer with his little brother, garden, and draw. Luz loves cooking as well. Since he was very young he has been helping his madre with dinner. Sometimes he catches a glimpse of what life in the United States could be like in magazines around town. He hopes that one day he can ride a jet ski or own a mountain bike. Luz dreams of owning his own gardening business in the United States and bringing his familia to California.

About the Author

Edward A. Dennis was born and raised in Phoenix, AZ. Edward worked for ten years as a public Special Education teacher in downtown Phoenix. He currently works as a game designer creating storyboard art and animations. In his free time Edward enjoys all types of cycling and outdoor activities. As a Mexican-American, Edward feels it's important for children to learn about tough issues regarding immigration. One of his biggest hopes is that children who look like him will be inspired by his artwork and learn more about the arts, or simply go out and ride a bike. Edward now lives in Los Angeles, CA.

DragonFruit, an imprint of Mango Publishing, publishes high-quality children's books to inspire a love of lifelong learning in readers. DragonFruit publishes a variety of titles for kids, including children's picture books, nonfiction series, toddler activity books, pre-K activity books, science and education titles, and ABC books. Beautiful and engaging, our books celebrate diversity, spark curiosity, and capture the imaginations of parents and children alike.

Mango Publishing, established in 2014, publishes an eclectic list of books by diverse authors. We were named the Fastest Growing Independent Publisher by Publishers Weekly in 2019 and 2020. Our success is bolstered by our main goal, which is to publish high-quality books that will make a positive impact in people's lives.

Our readers are our most important resource; we value your input, suggestions, and ideas. We'd love to hear from you—after all, we are publishing books for you!

Please stay in touch with us and follow us at:
Instagram: @dragonfruitkids
Facebook: Mango Publishing
Twitter: @MangoPublishing
LinkedIn: Mango Publishing
Pinterest: Mango Publishing

Sign up for our newsletter at www.mangopublishinggroup.com and receive a free book! Join us on Mango's journey to change publishing, one book at a time.

CPSIA information can be obtained
at www.ICGtesting.com
Printed in the USA
JSHW011857191122
33511JS00003B/8